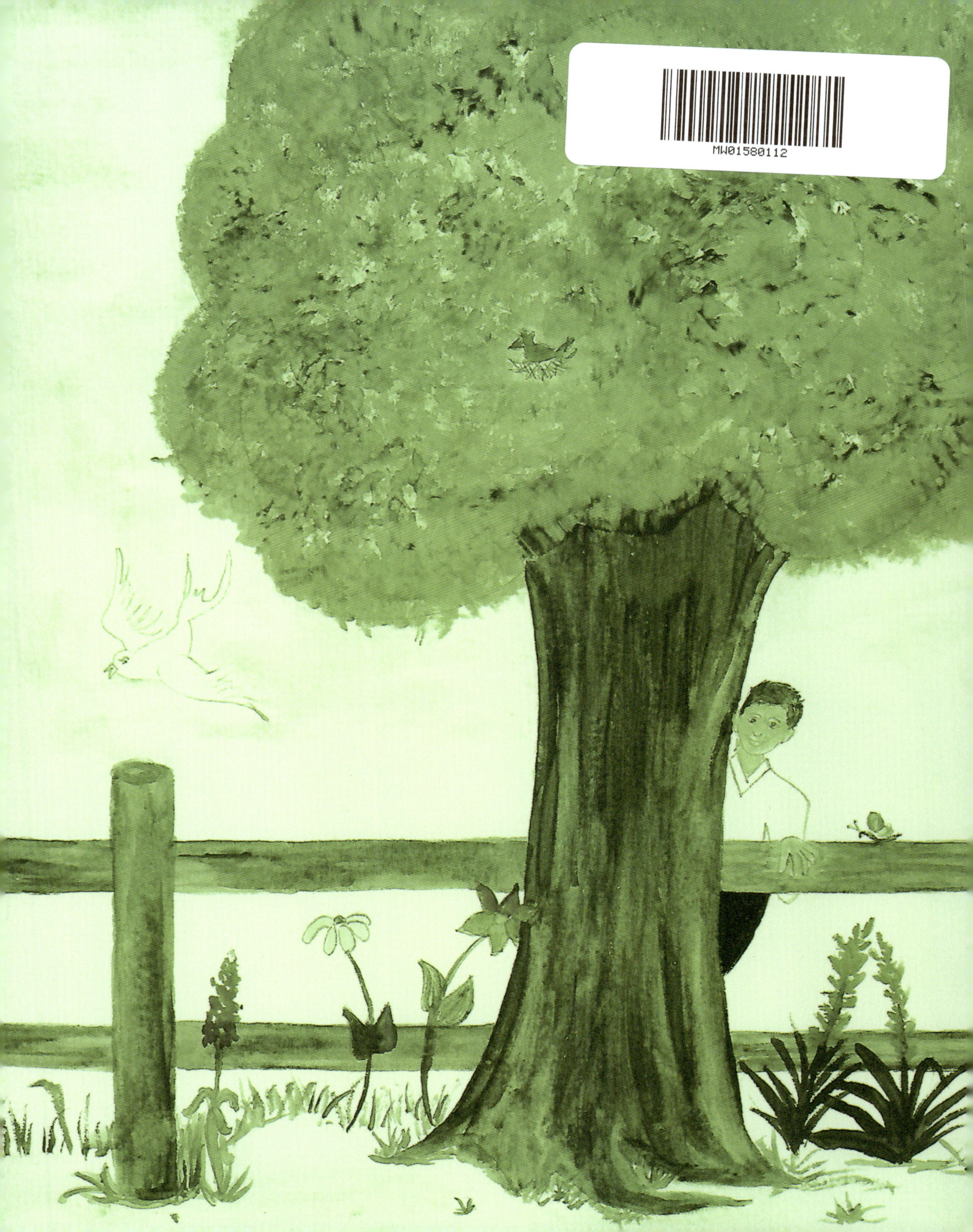

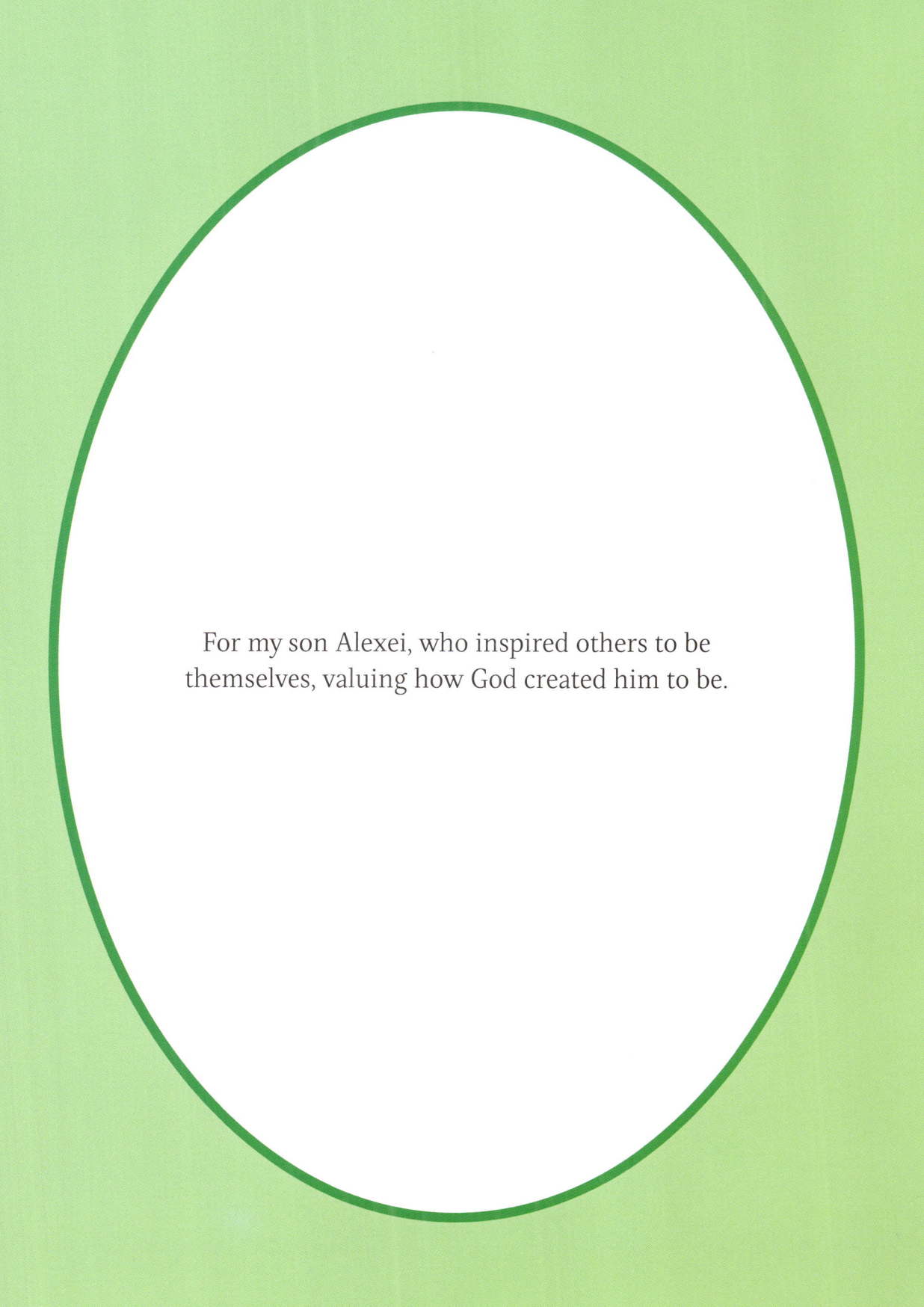

For my son Alexei, who inspired others to be themselves, valuing how God created him to be.

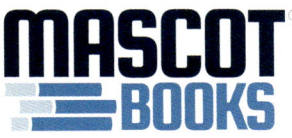

www.mascotbooks.com

Things We Wish to Say

©2019 Anna Bauereis. All Rights Reserved. No part of this publication may be reproduced, stored in a retrieval system or transmitted in any form by any means electronic, mechanical, or photocopying, recording or otherwise without the permission of the author.

For more information, please contact:
Mascot Books
620 Herndon Parkway, Suite 320
Herndon, VA 20170
info@mascotbooks.com

Library of Congress Control Number: 2019947670

CPSIA Code: PRT0919A
ISBN-13: 978-0-578-54222-5

Printed in the United States

Things We Wish To Say

Anna Bauereis
Written by Alexei Bauereis
Illustrated by Kathy Carpenter

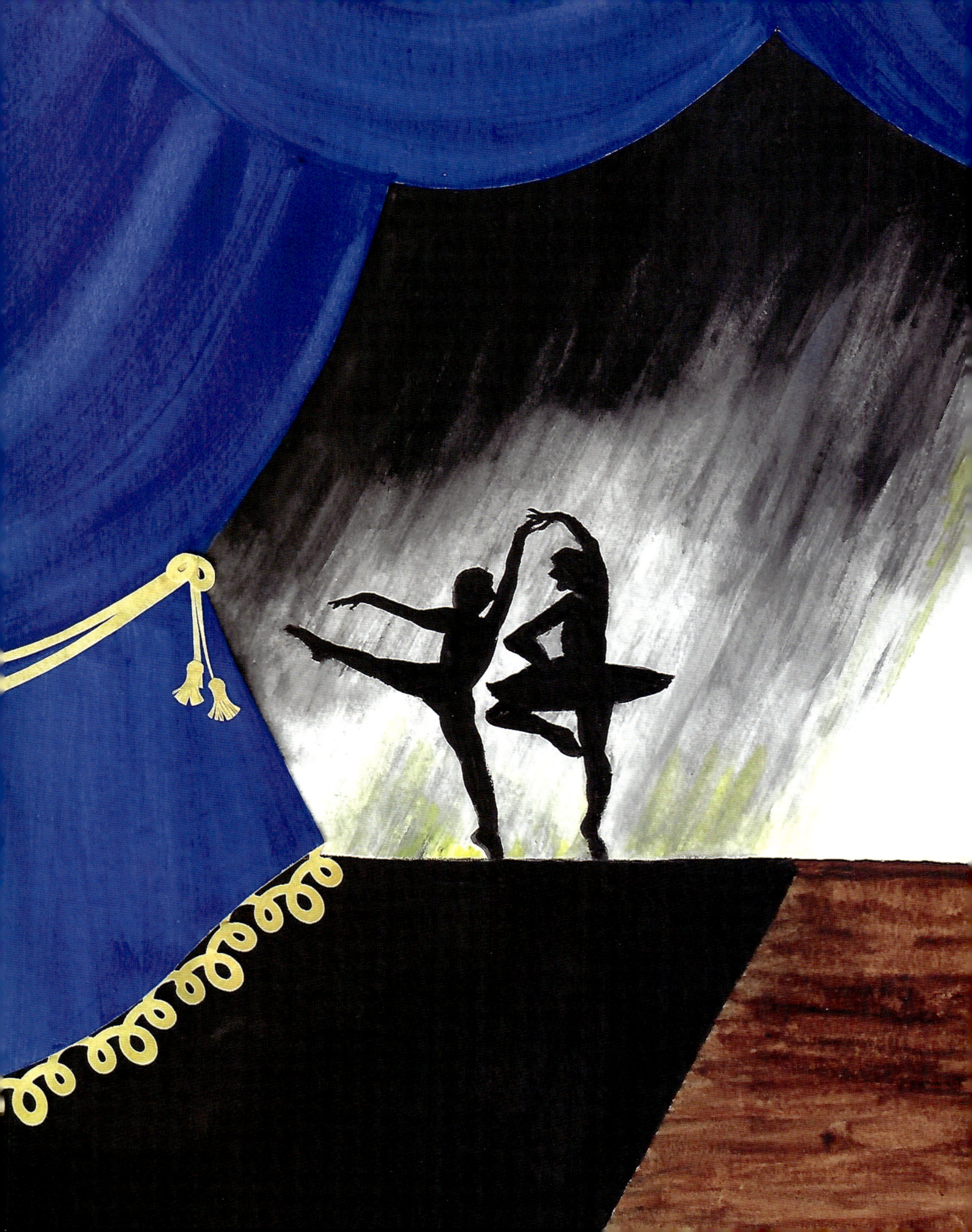

The things we wish to say...

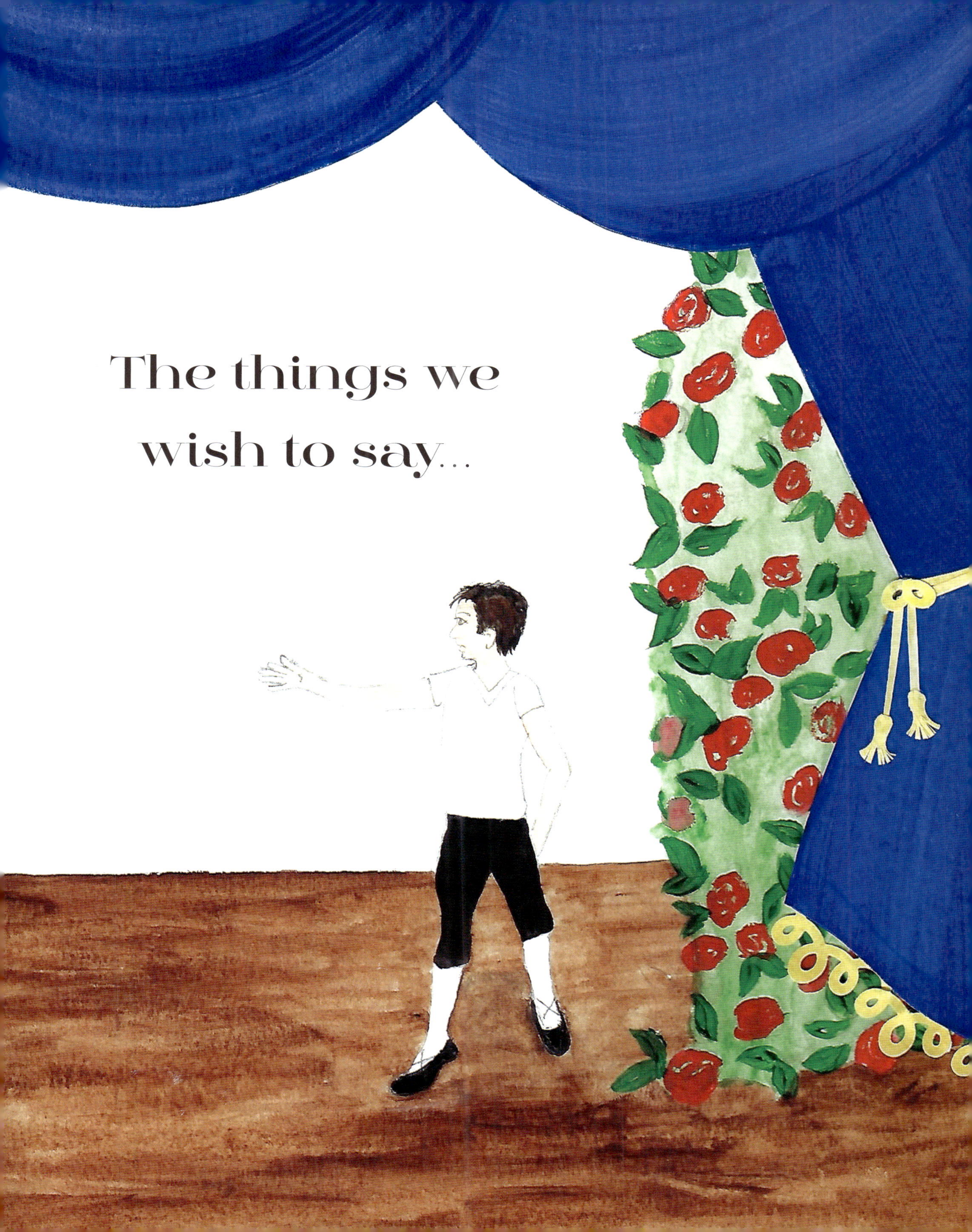

If only the thoughts
we think

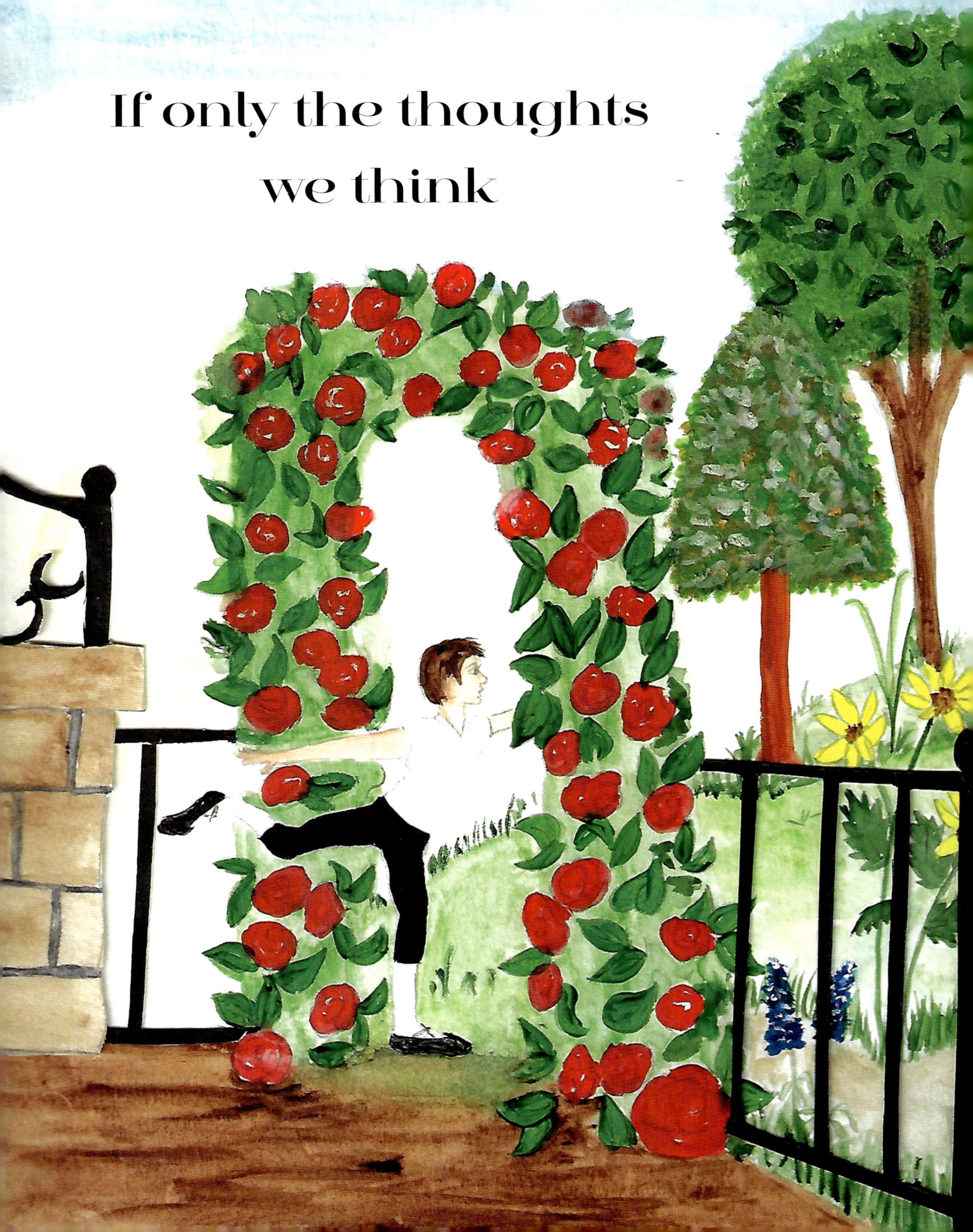

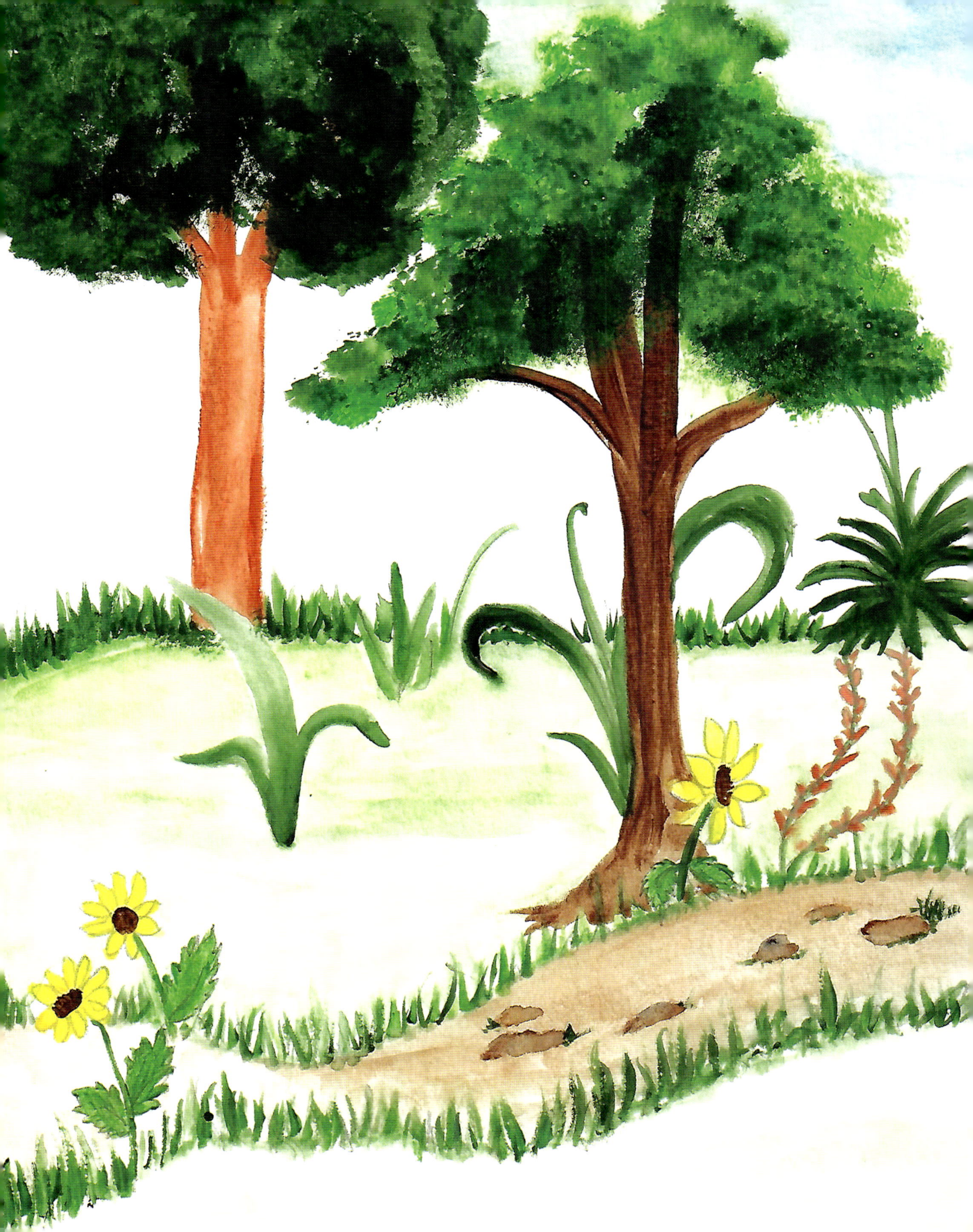

Came out of our mouths.

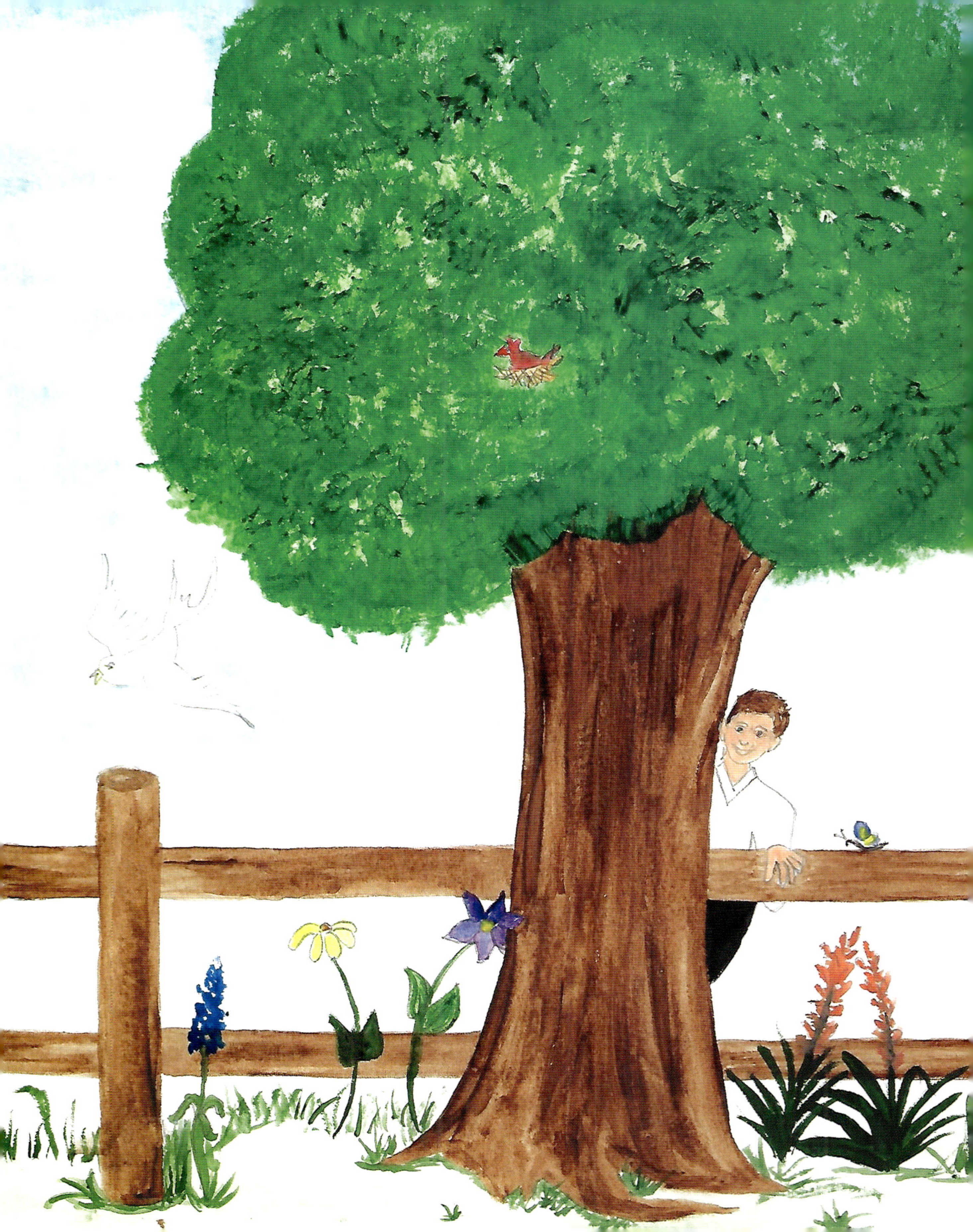

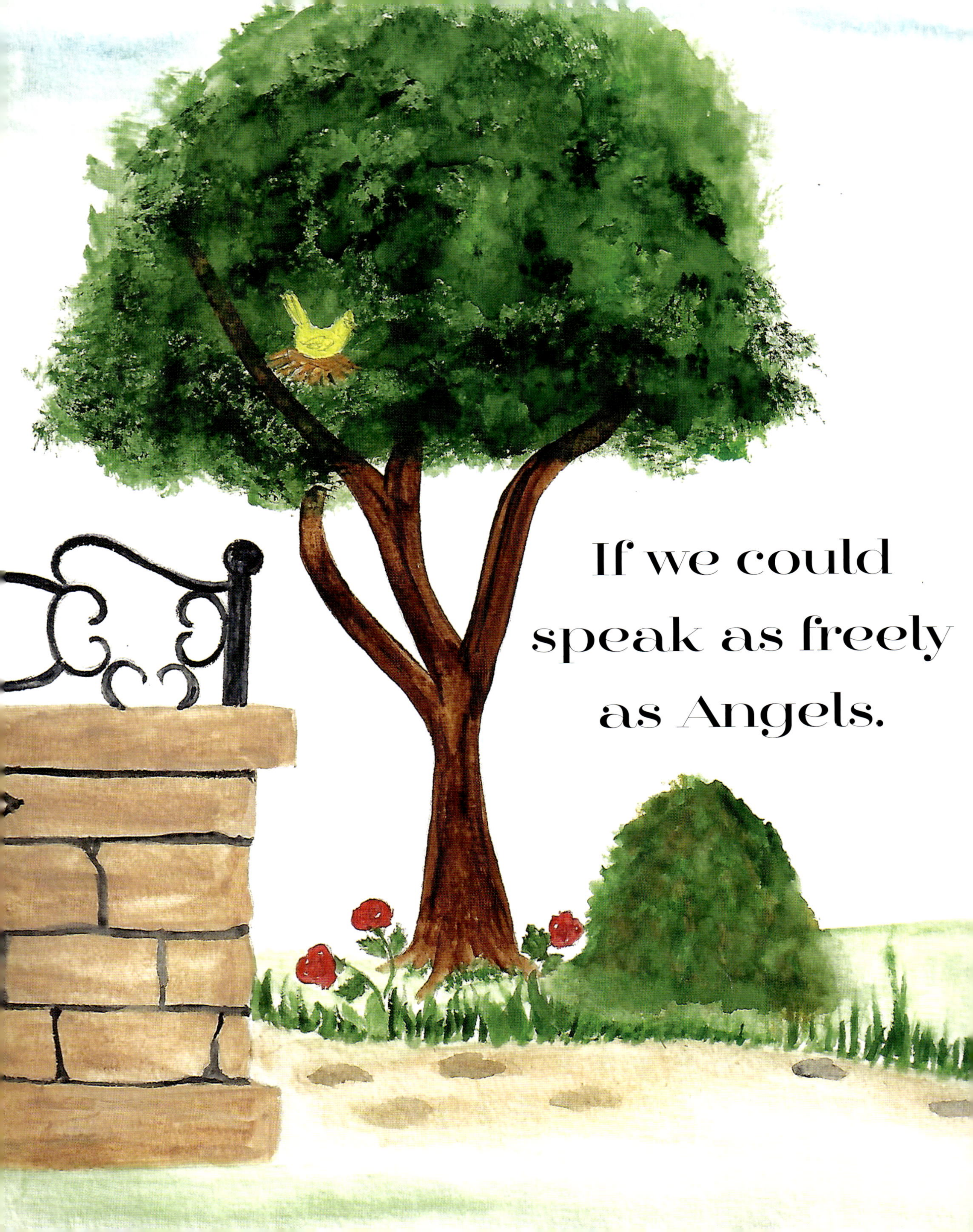

If we could
speak as freely
as Angels.

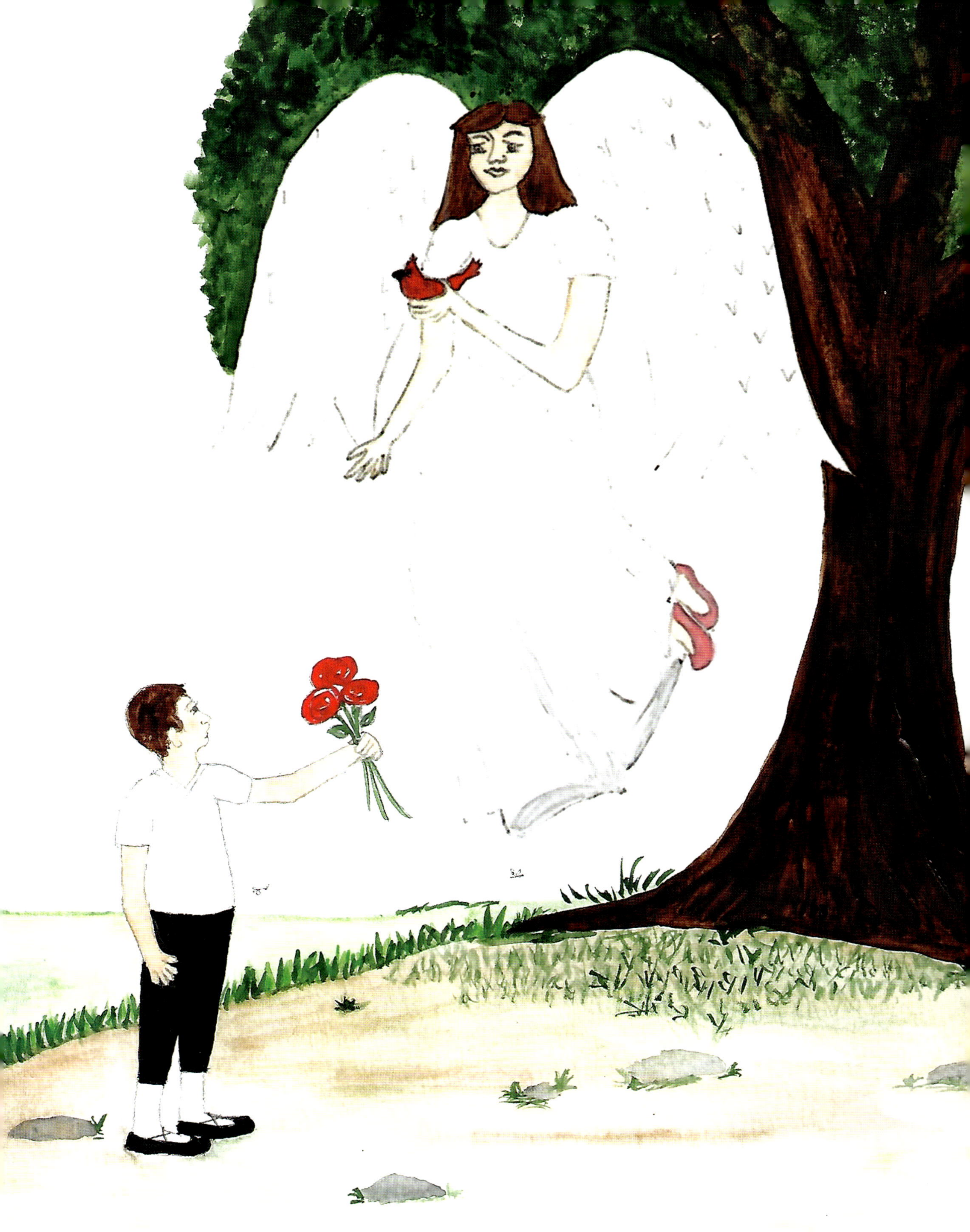

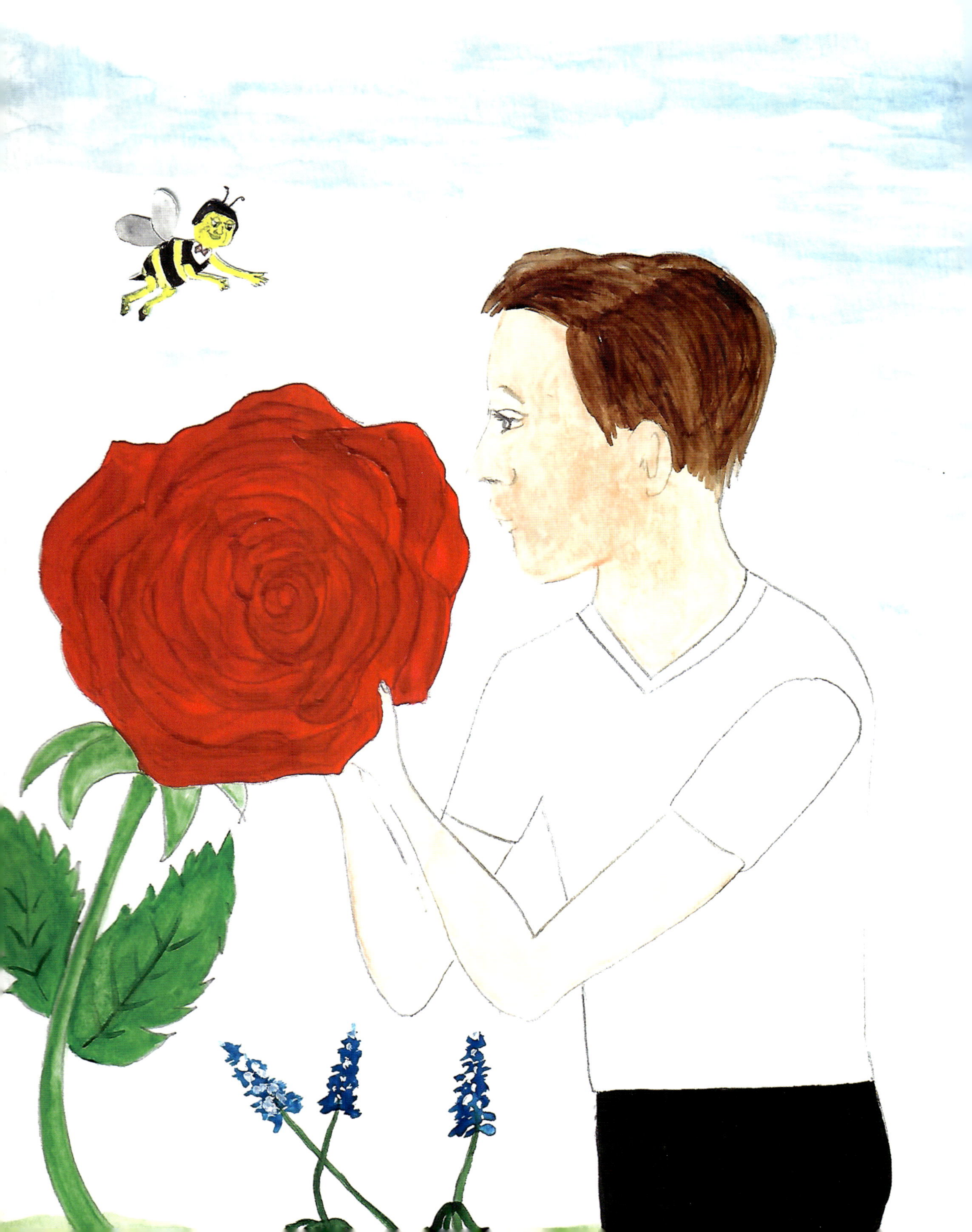

Things we wish we
could say freely,

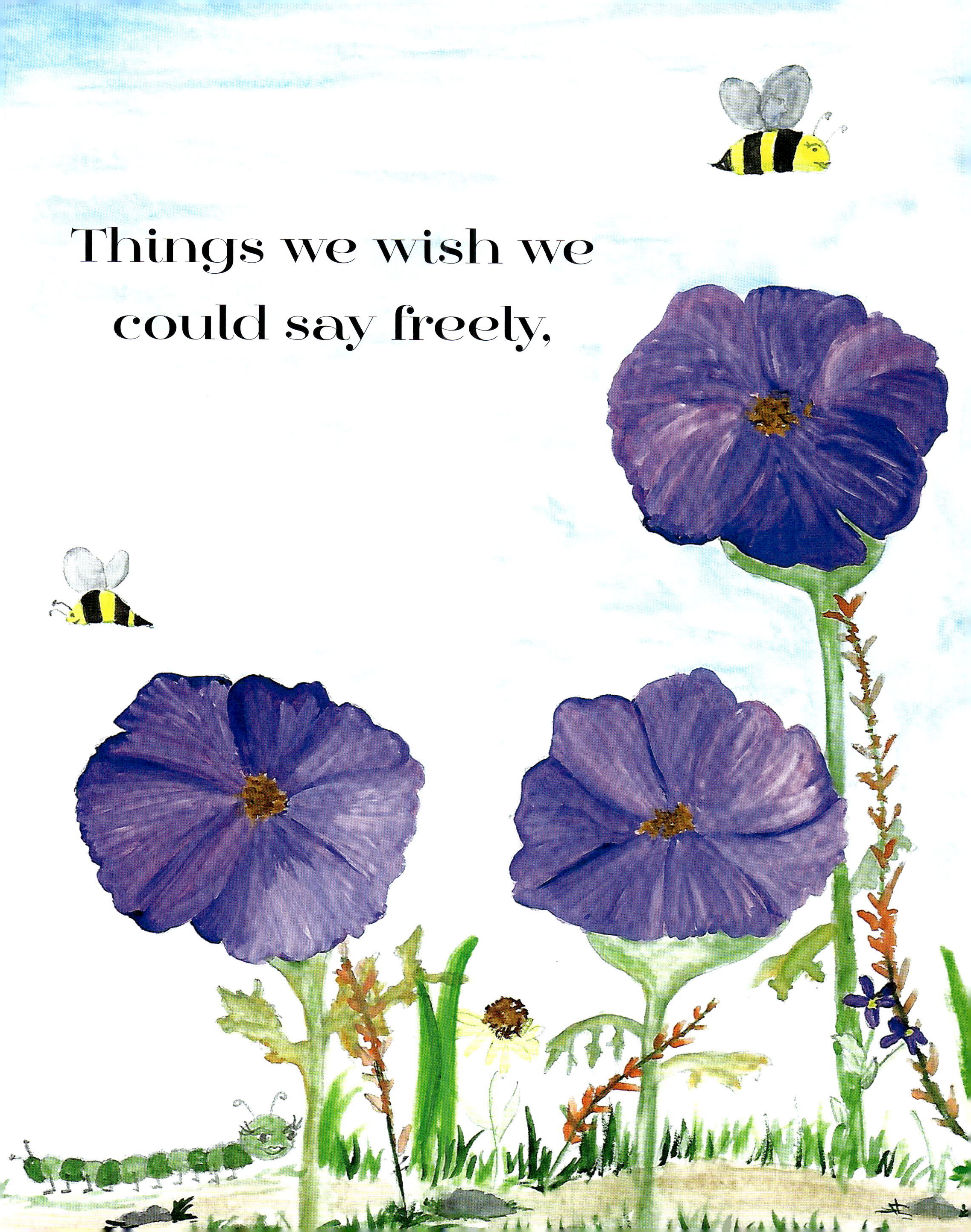

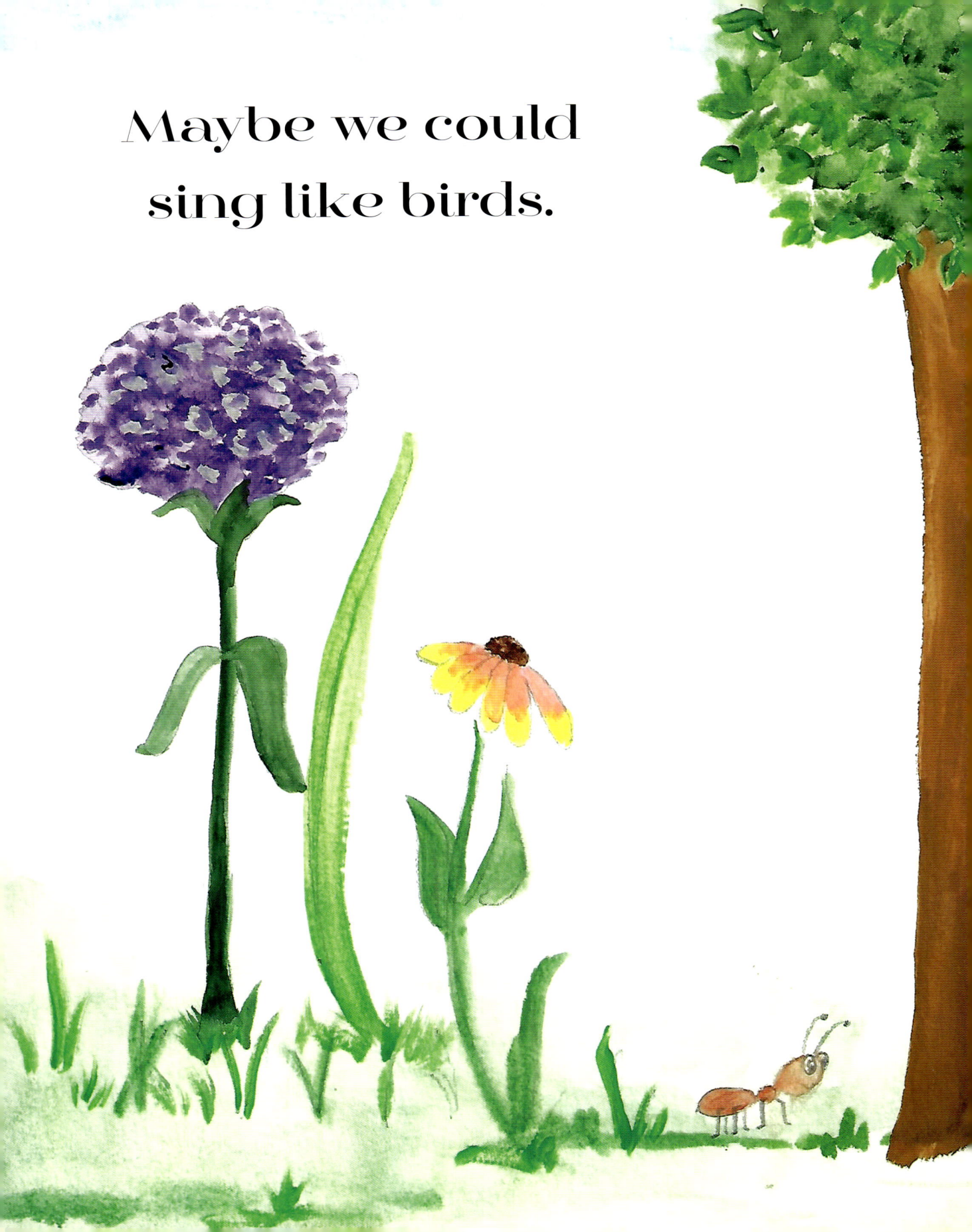

Maybe we could
sing like birds.

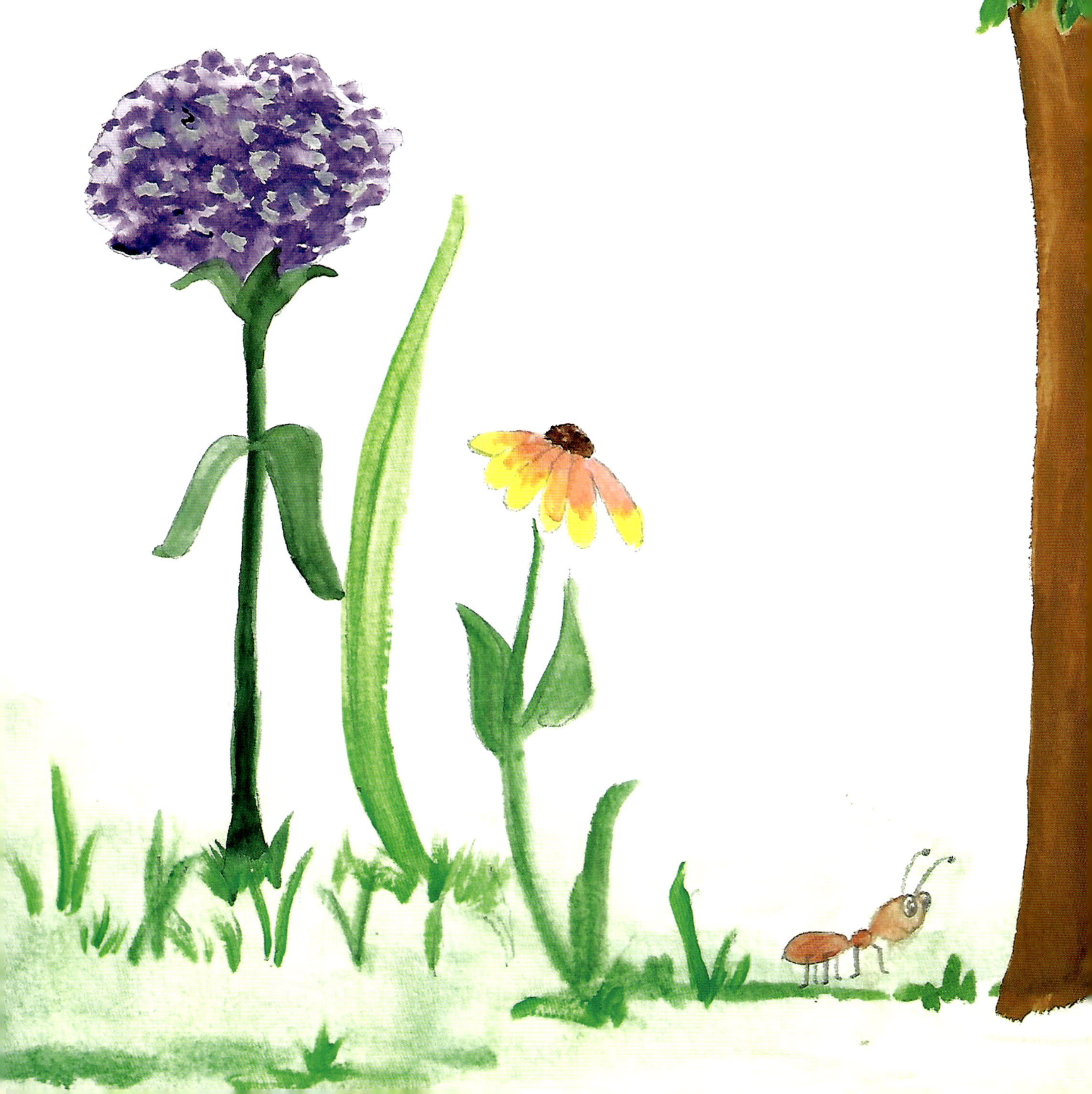

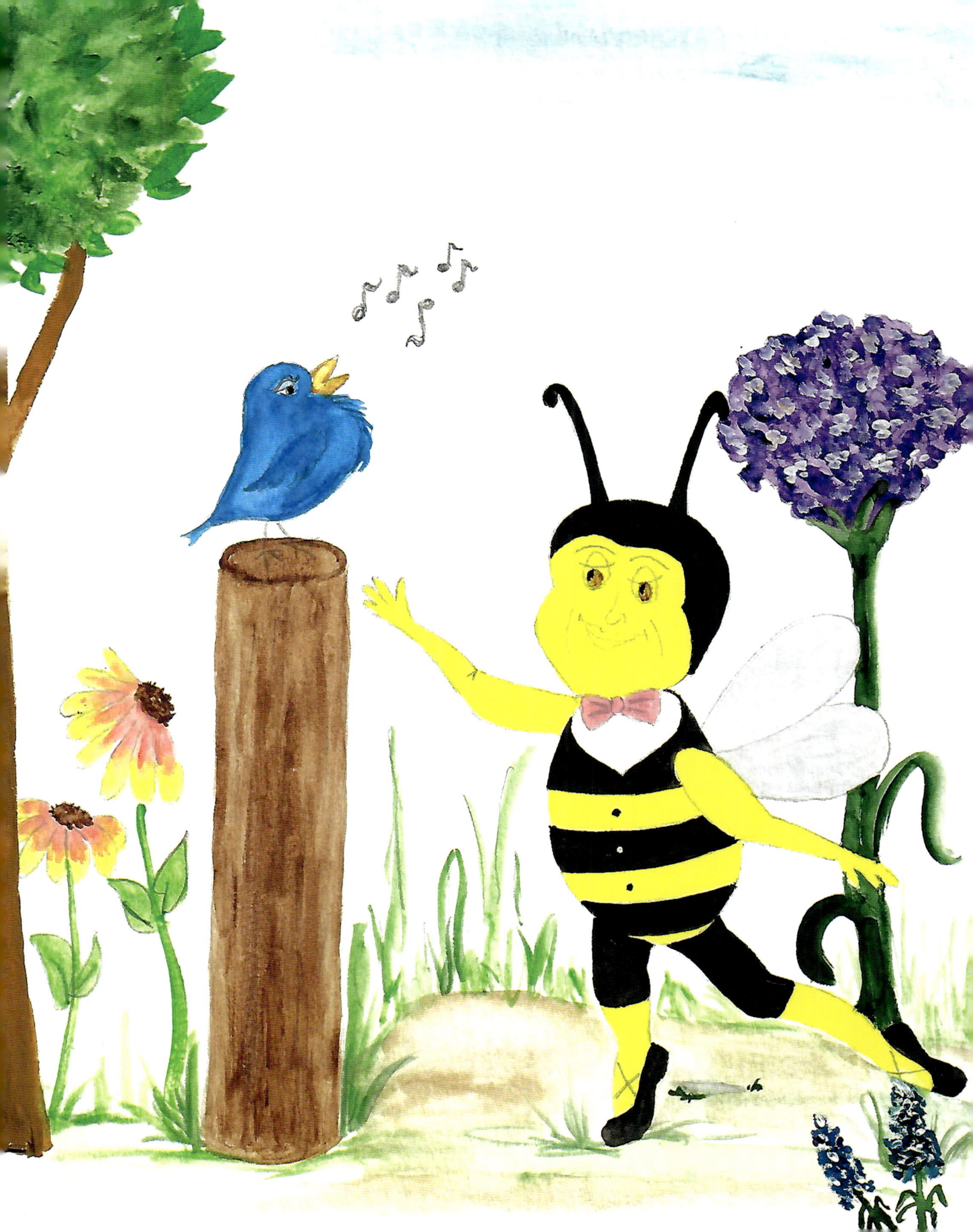

Sing to say what we want.

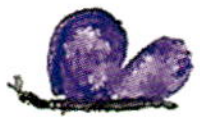

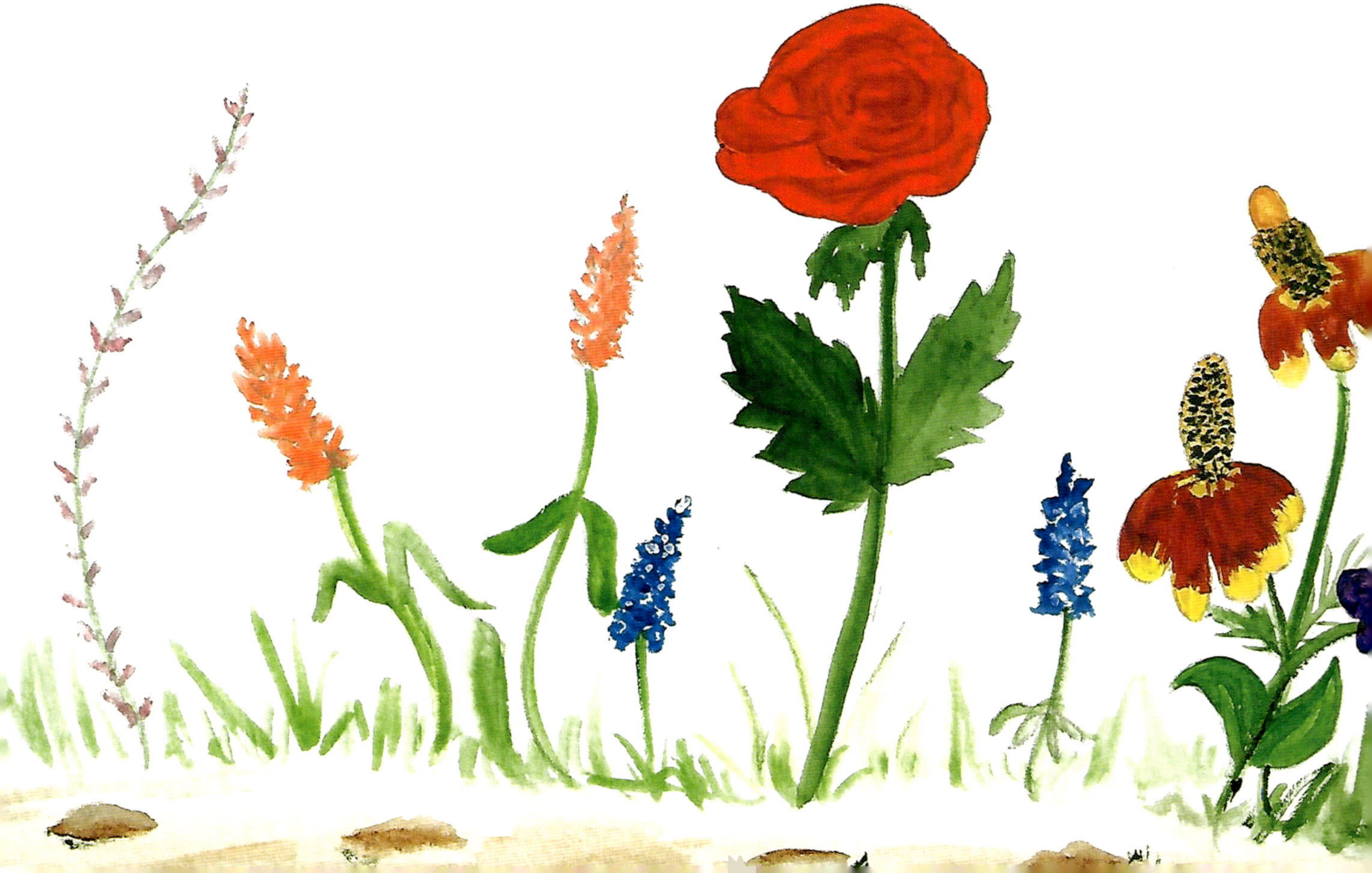

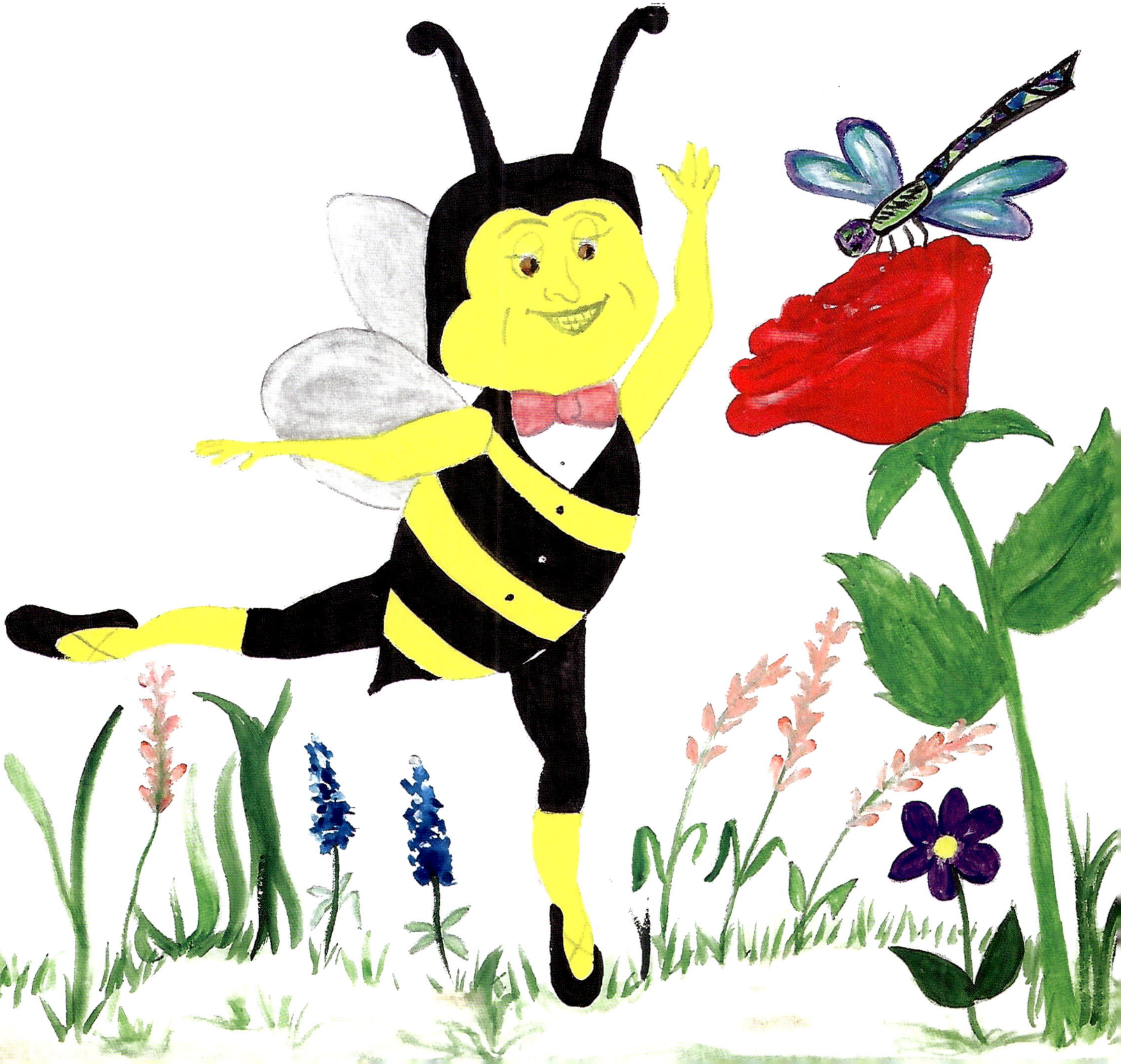

Maybe
it's through dance.

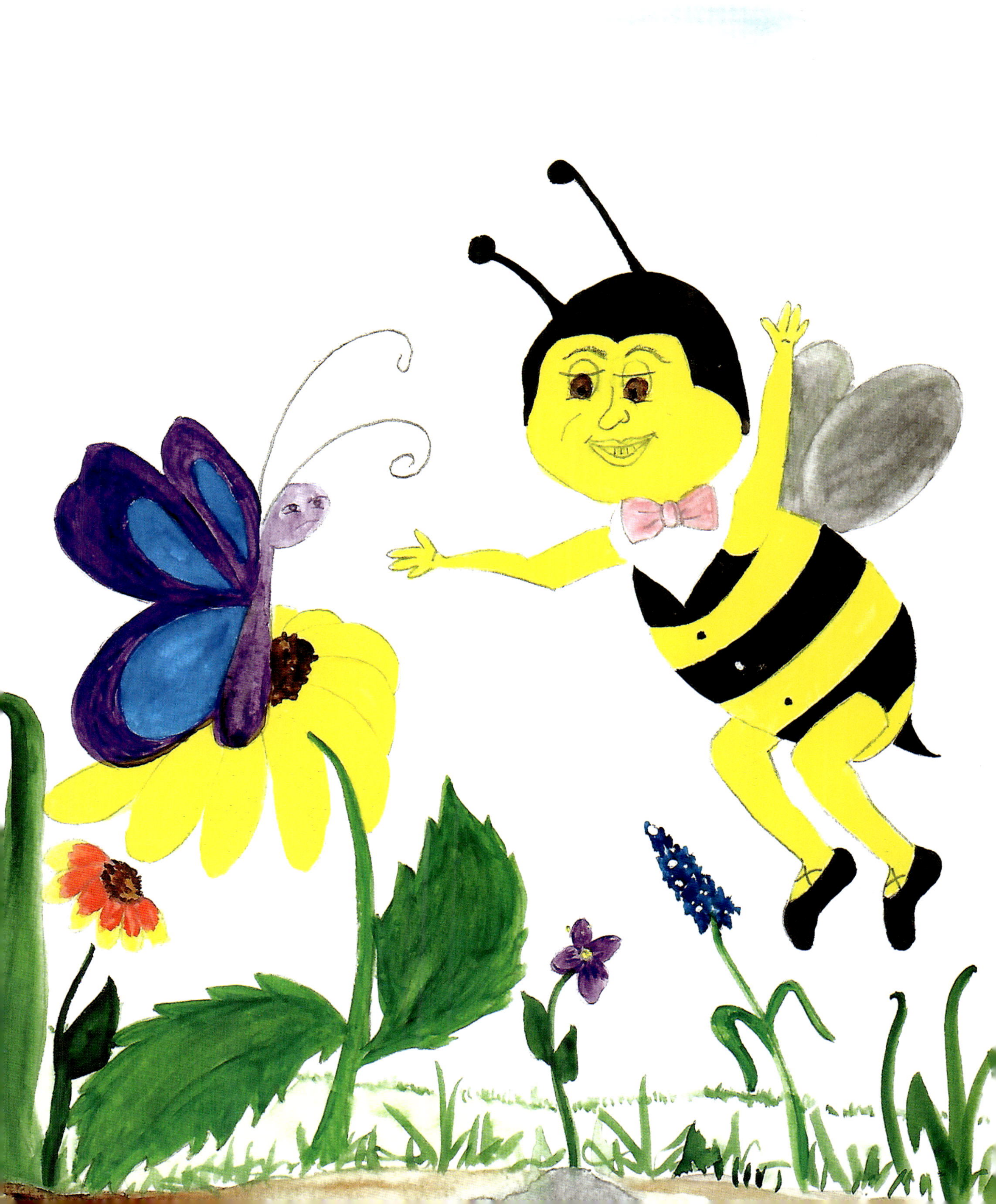

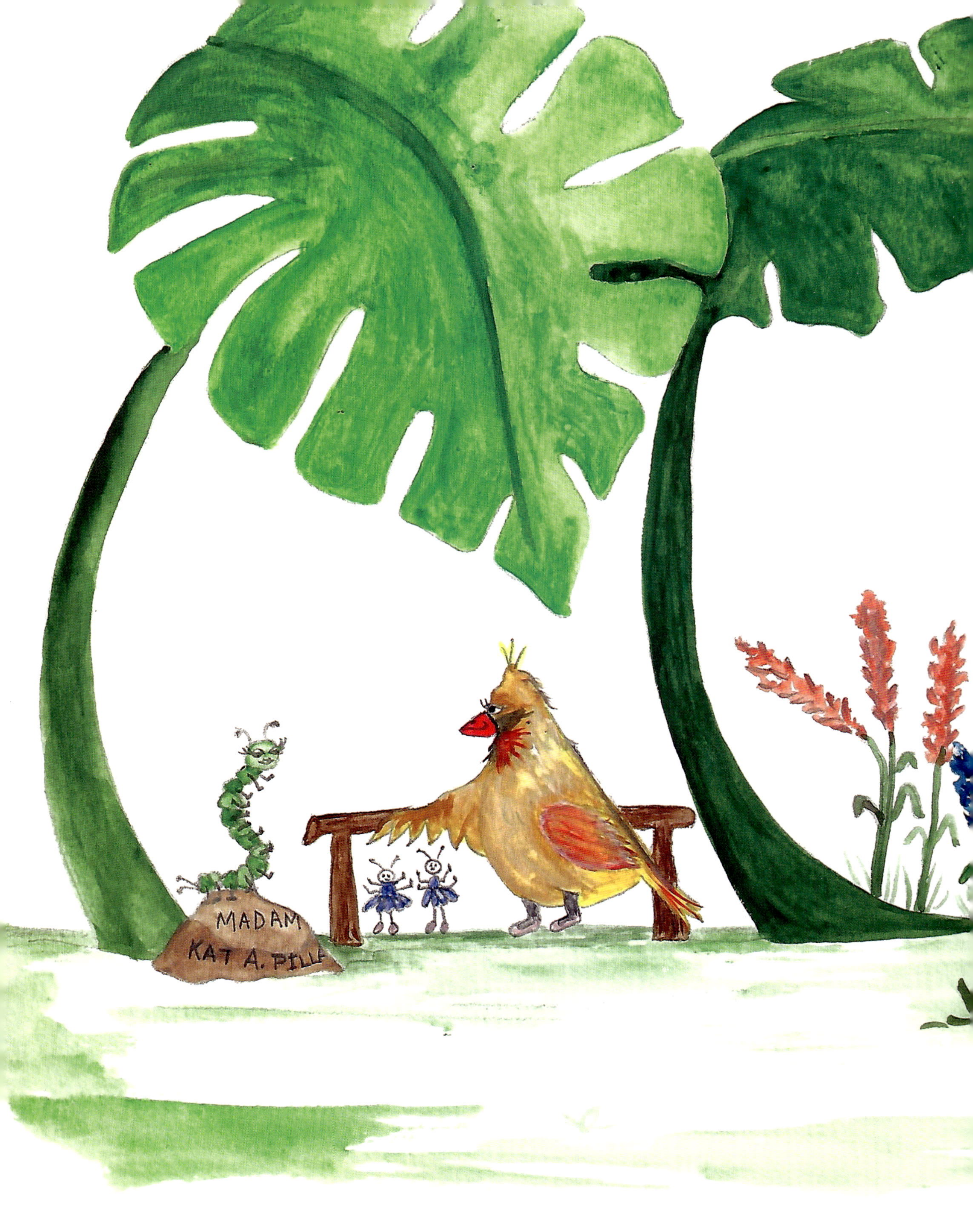
MADAM
KAT A. PILL

If we could
dance like

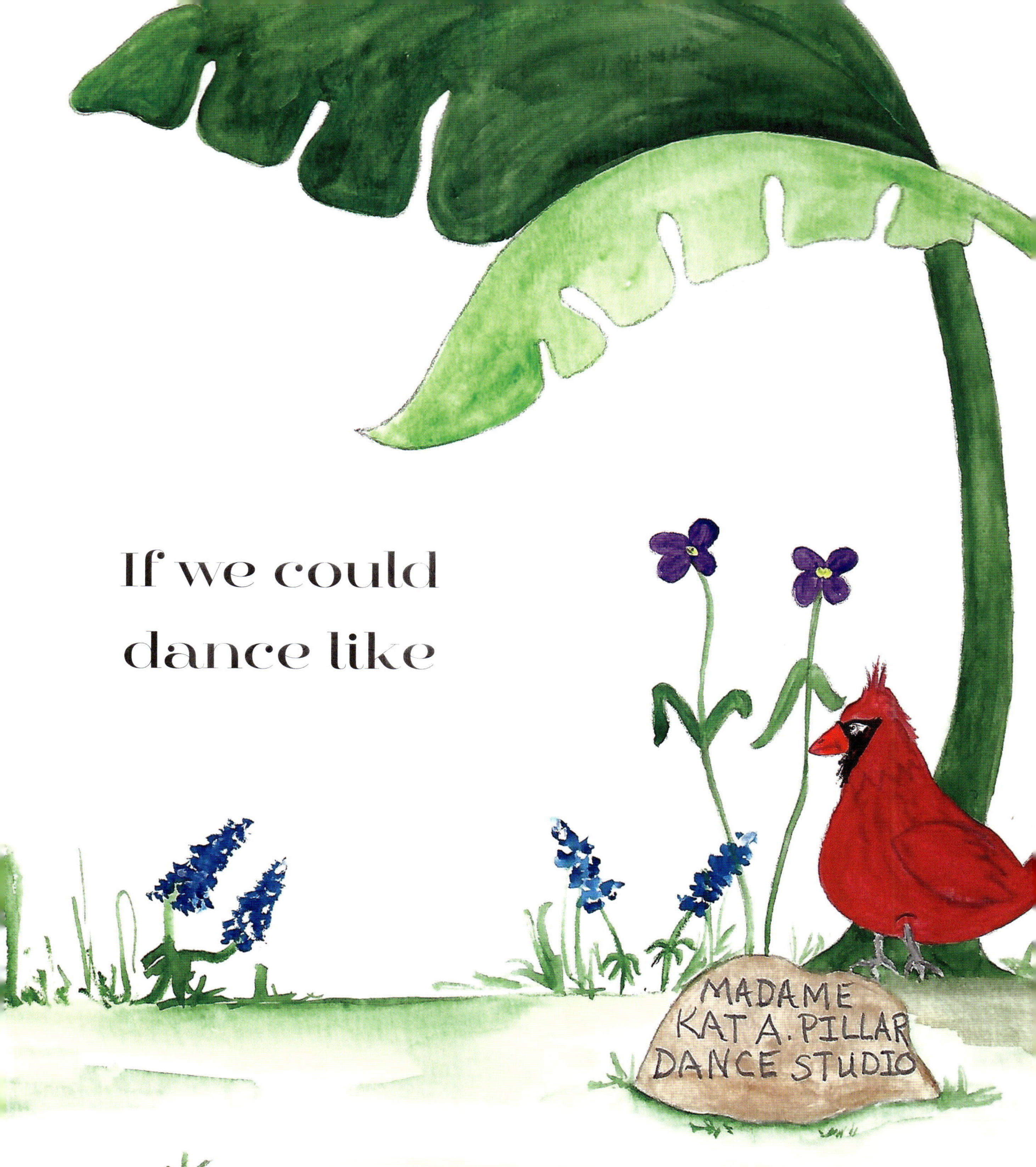
MADAME
KAT A. PILLAR
DANCE STUDIO

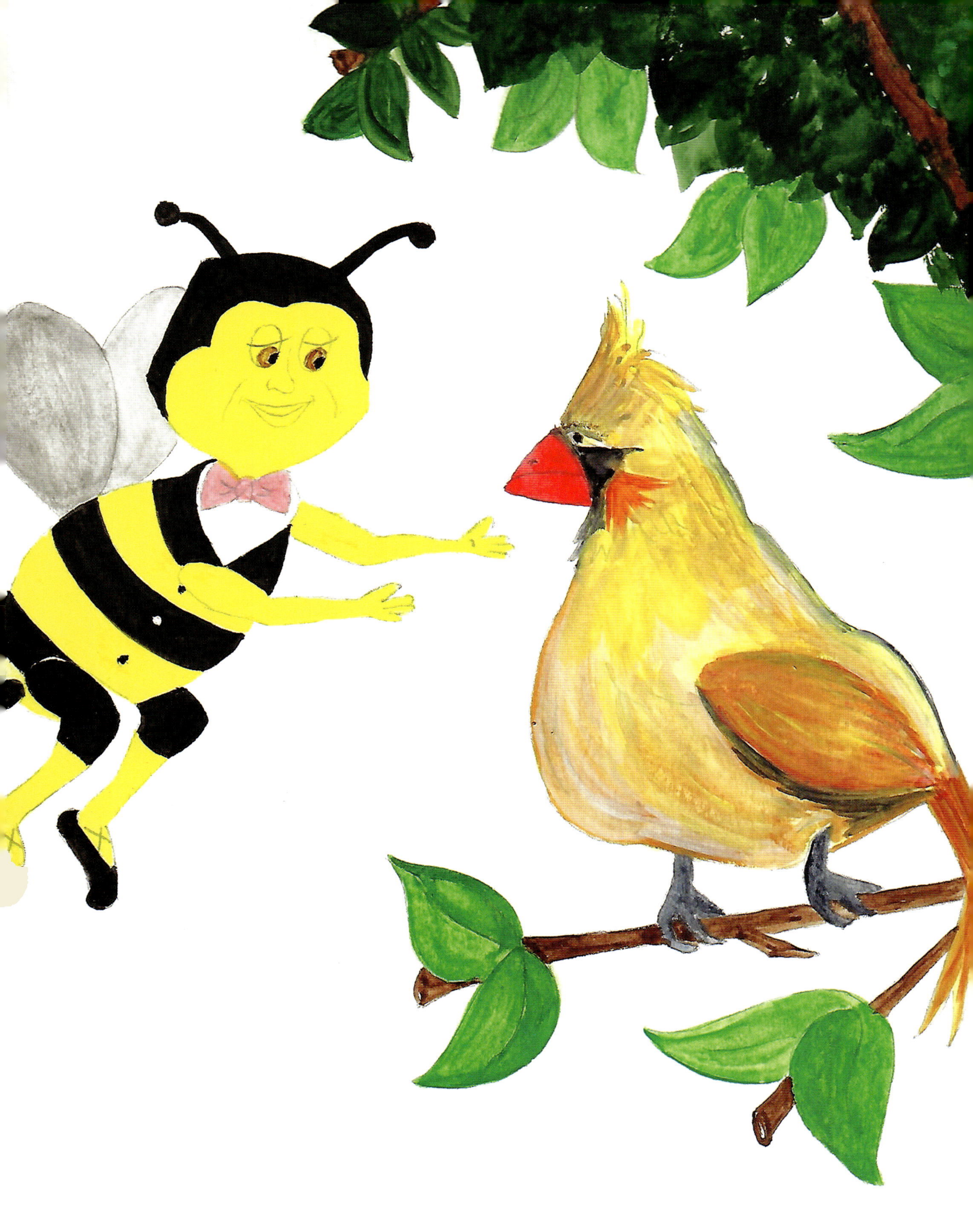

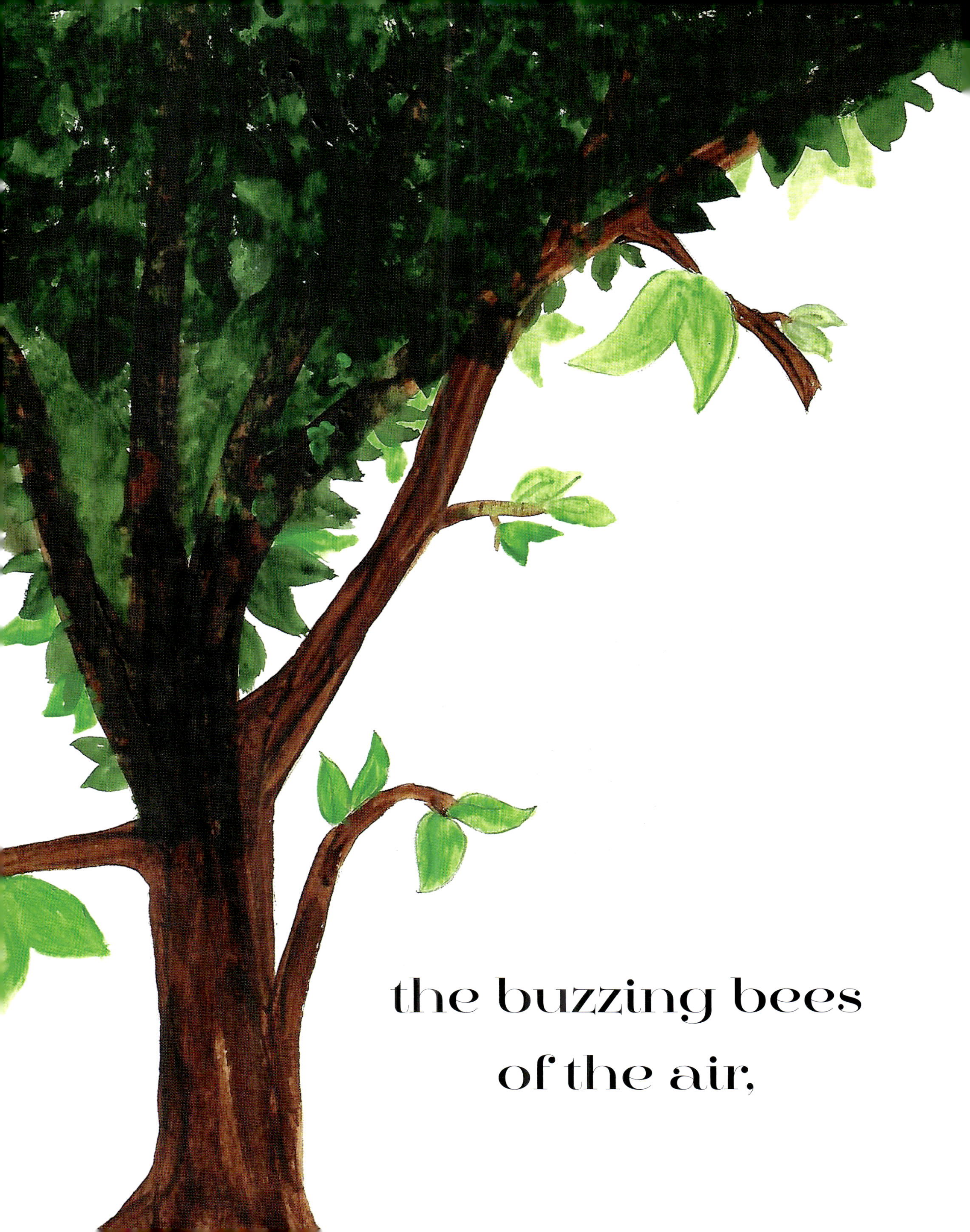

the buzzing bees
of the air,

To say what we want.

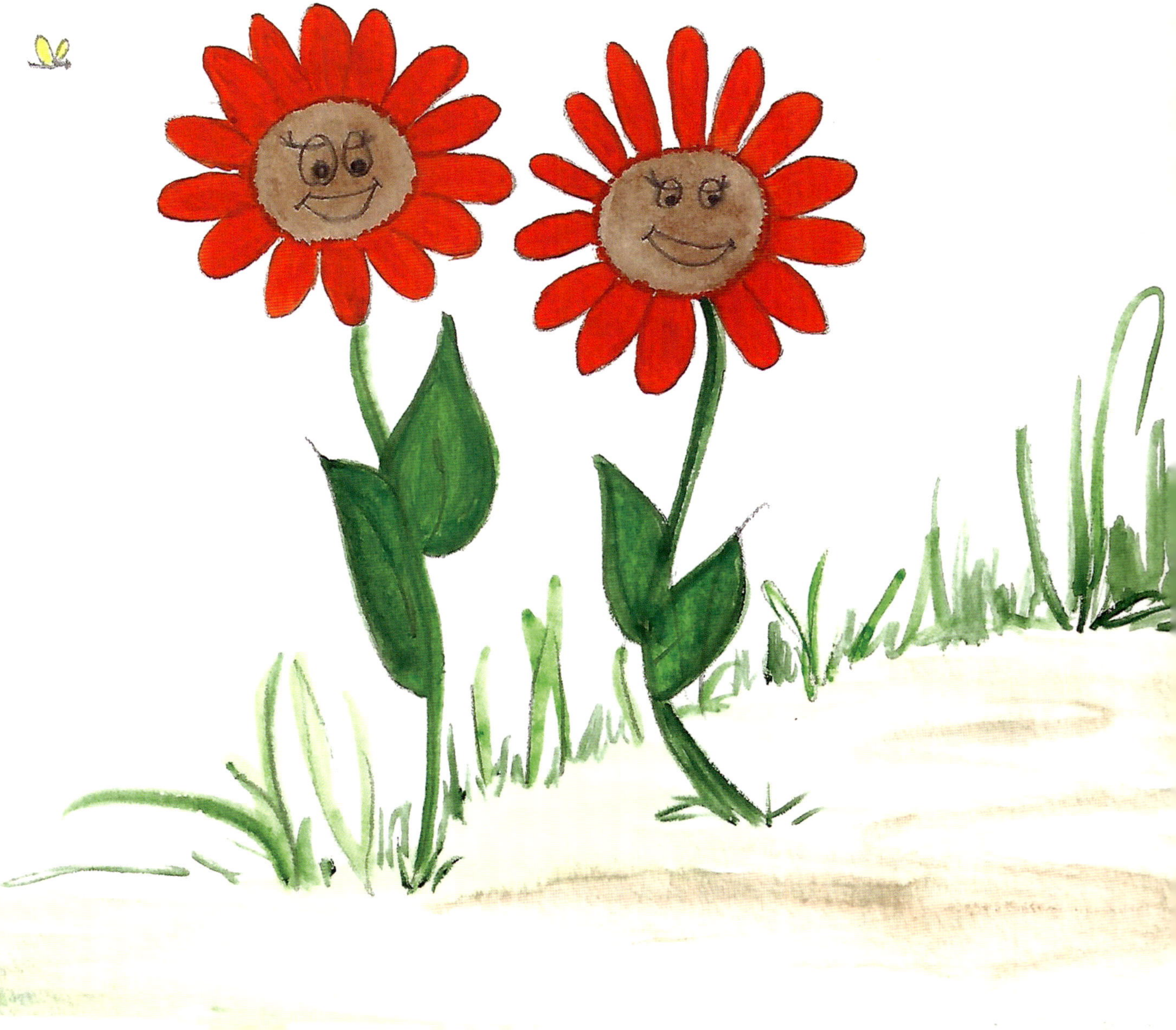

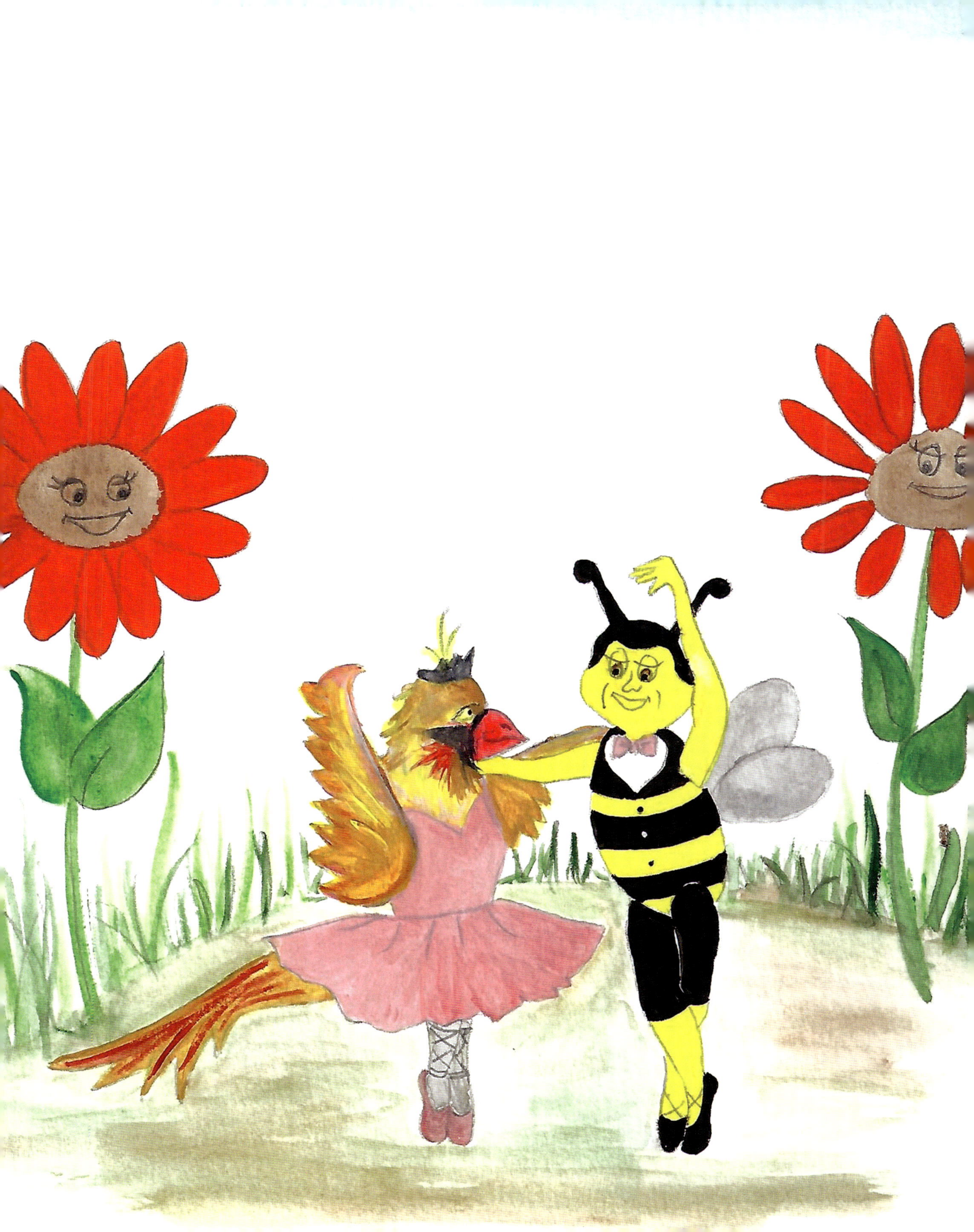

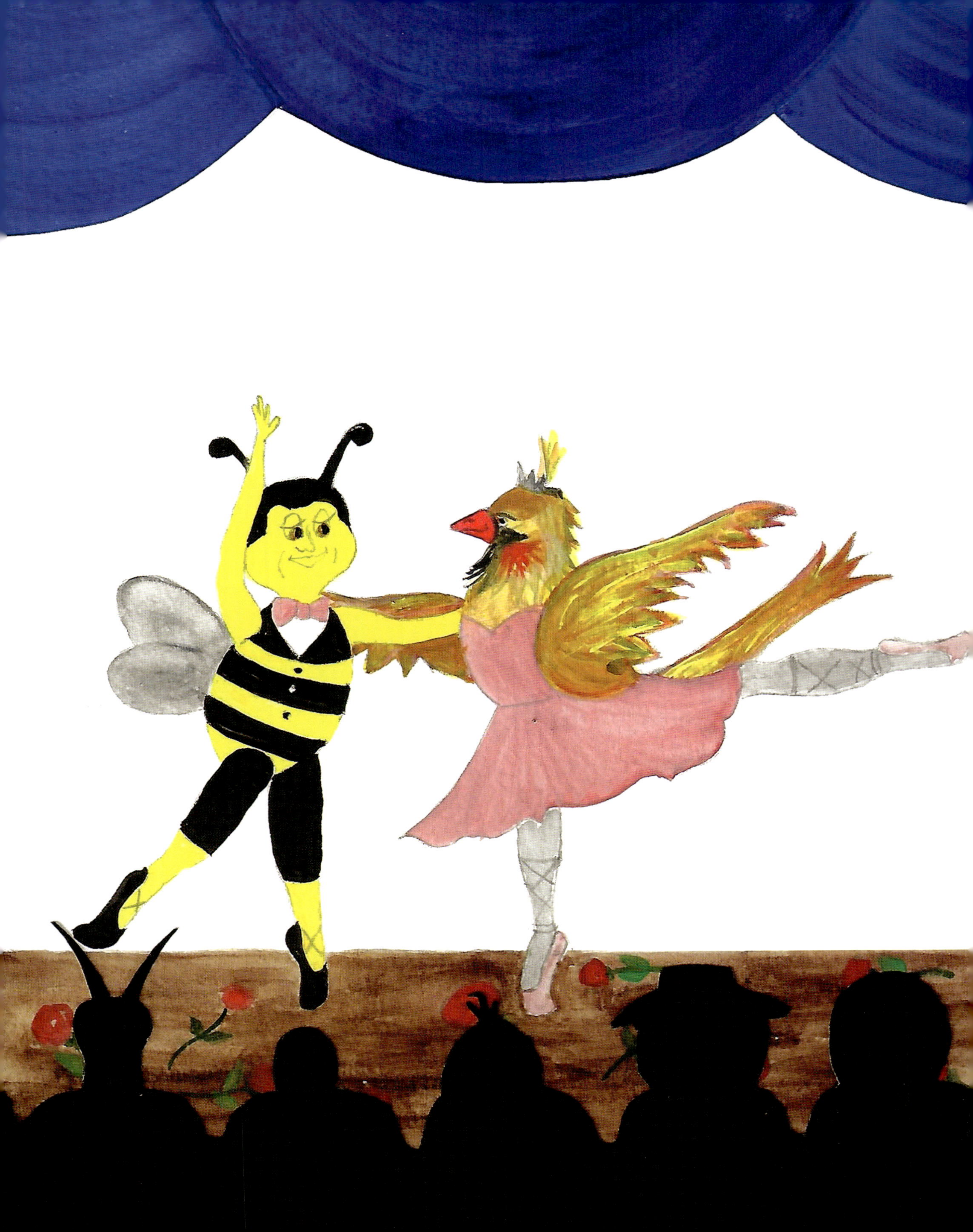

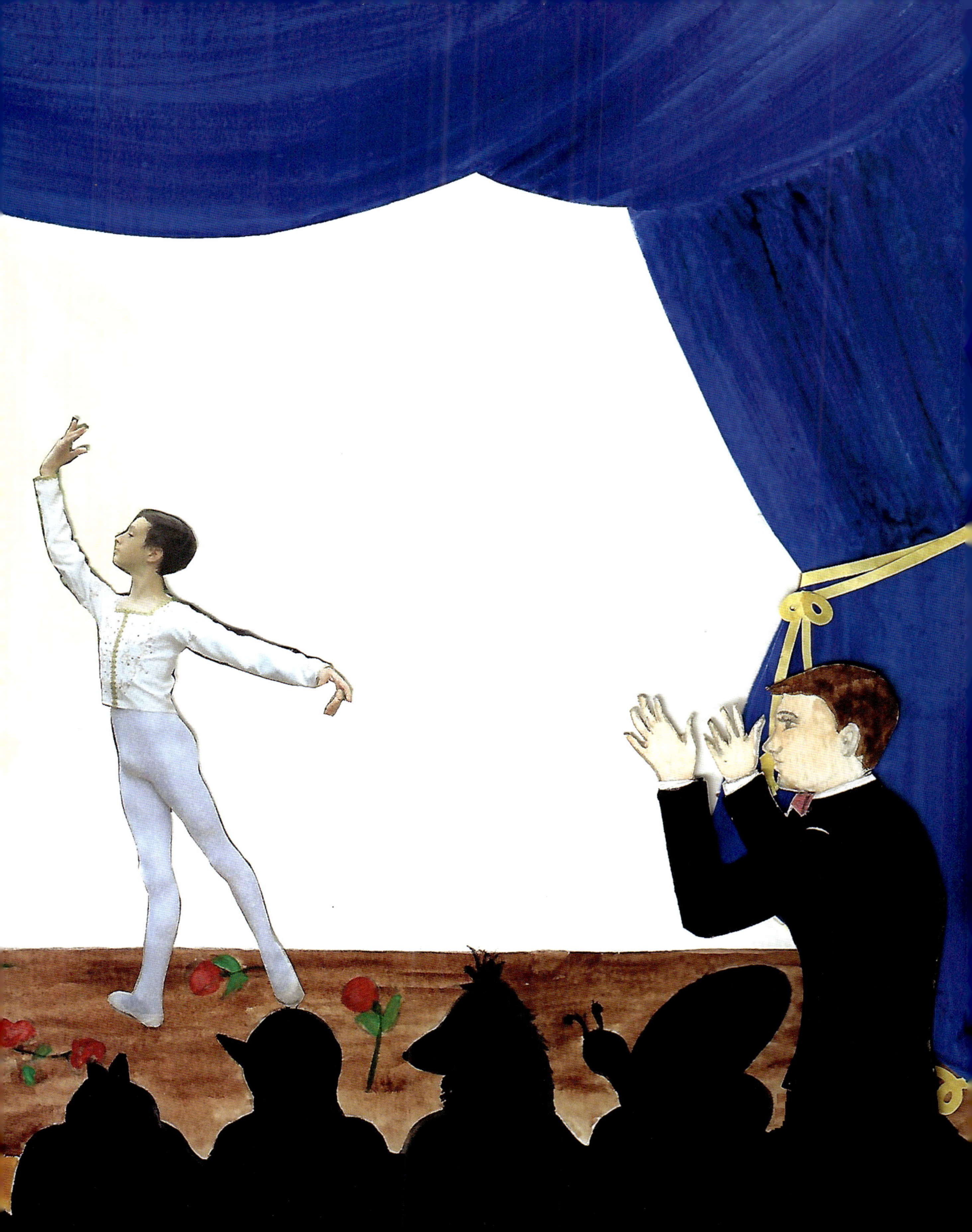

About Anna

With expertise across a wide and diverse range of industries and success driven by passion, Anna Bauereis brings a powerful piece of her heart to the world. This is evidenced by her latest endeavor: her beautiful new children's book, *Things We Wish to Say.*

After experiencing the grief of losing her beloved son, Alexei, the outpouring of love toward her and her family revealed the influence of a godly gentleman who made an impact beyond his short fourteen years of life. Anna is launching a series of books that will serve as starting points for conversations between dancers and their parents for the purpose of discussing the experiences and attitudes about their passion for dance and their place in their community. By the grace of God and an unstoppable spirit, Anna has made it her personal mission to make a difference in the lives of others and, most importantly, to help you find joy.

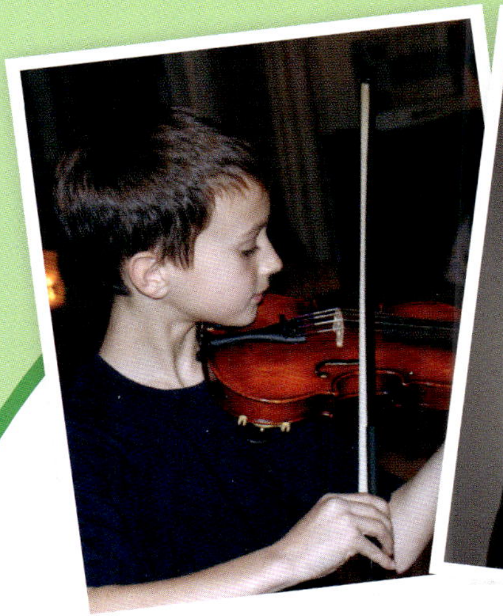

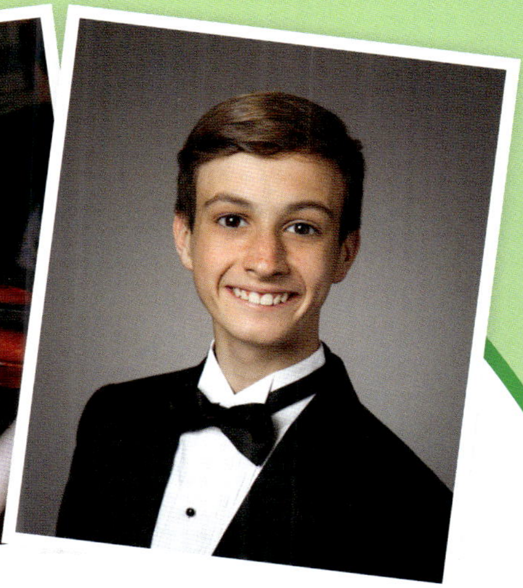

About Alexei

Friends and family say Alexei was a very special young man who left a life-long impression and a true legacy of joy and love. He was a young man whose love and exuberance for life were always apparent, but never as much as when he was dancing. While his life off the dance floor was, at times, challenging, he found ways to overcome it all. Alexei's permanent smile and unwavering optimism was what drew people to him and what gave him the ability to express in movement more emotion than words ever could.

Alexei's love for life and dance will live on in all the people whose lives he touched. "Things We Wish to Say" is a poem Alexei wrote.

About the Illustrator

Kathy L. Carpenter is an author and illustrator of stories for children. She grew up in San Antonio, Texas, before moving to the Hill Country. Always drawing, she landed her dream job as the local H.E.B. Grocery artist, where she worked until her second child was born. Her displays hung in the store for many years.

After finding the love of her life, Carl, she finished college and has run several businesses. Kathy lives in the Hill Country with her wonderful husband and son. She is a mother of five, grandmother of eleven, and a great-grandmother of three.

This is her first illustration project with Mascot Books.

"God draws and lets me
hold the pencil."
— KC

Symbolism Key

Pink Bow Tie - Alexei really liked dark pink, but he was colorblind, so we are not sure what he saw

Blue Bonnets - Alexei was a Texan, born and raised, and they are everywhere just like Alexei

Red Roses - Alexei loved dark red roses

Daisies - His mom, Anna's, favorite flower

Musical Notes - The notes the birds are singing are from a song written by Ethan Rink and Desirea Caso

Cardinal Bird - Our grandmother's favorite bird

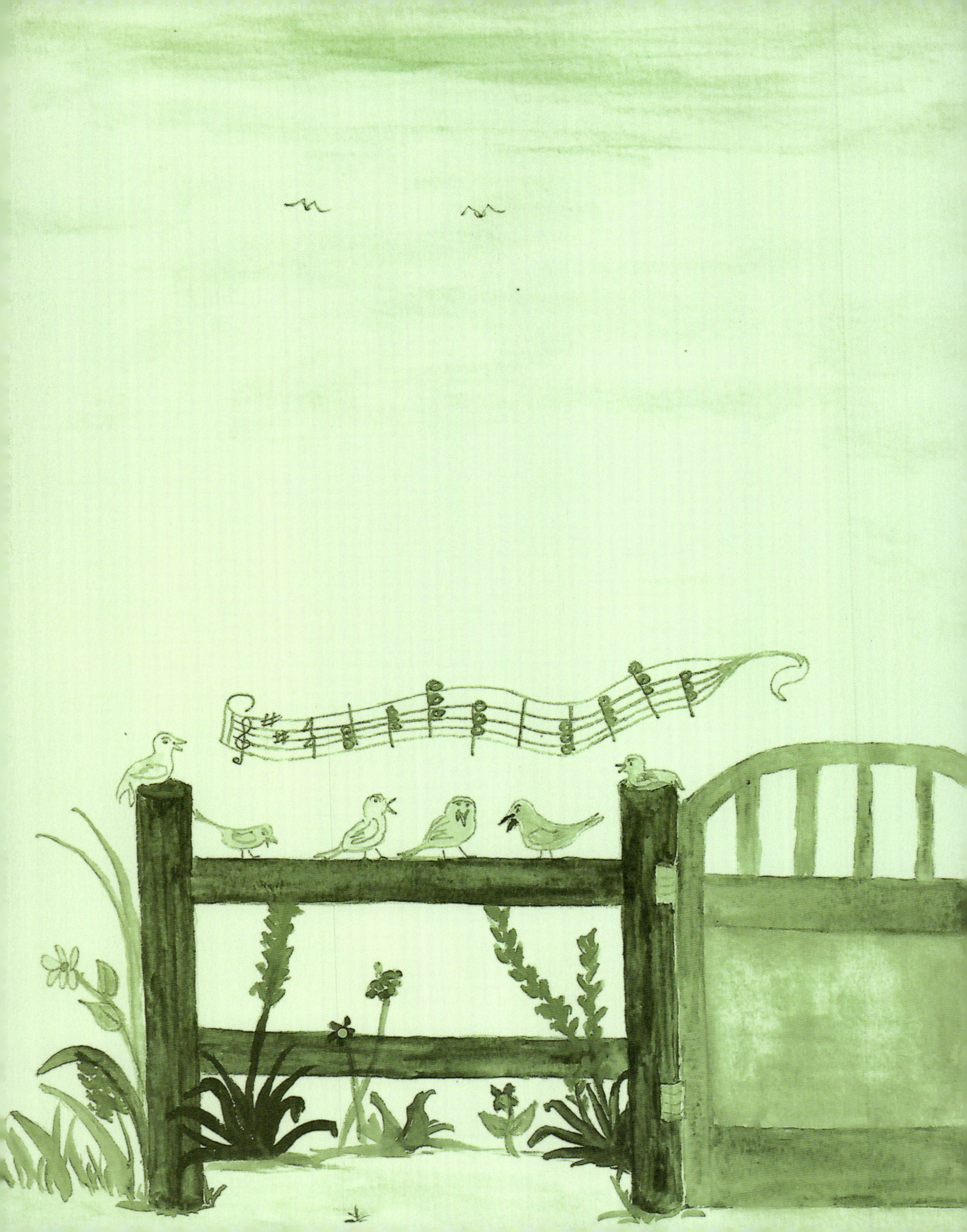

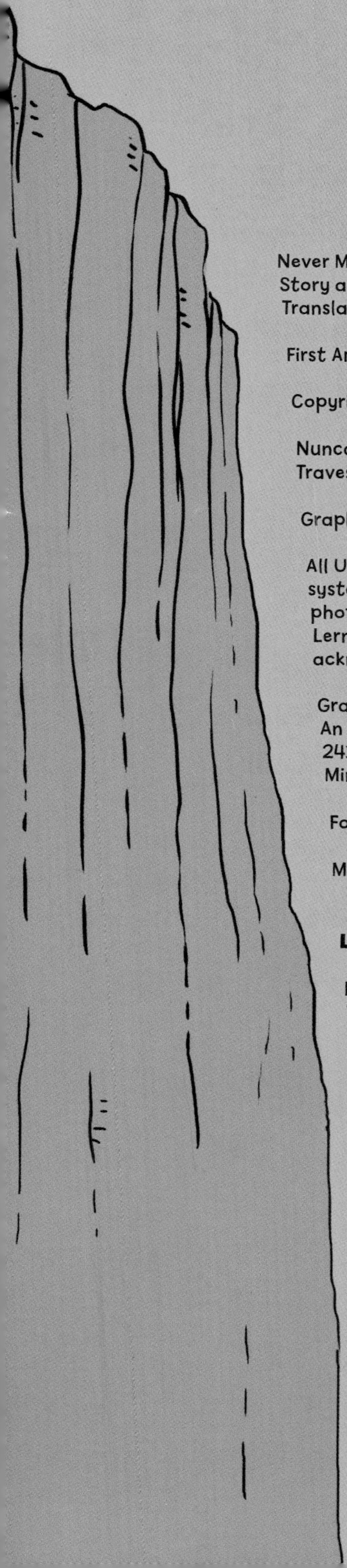

Never Make a Giant Mad
Story and illustrations by Artur Laperla
Translation by Norwyn MacTire

First American edition published in 2022 by Graphic Universe™

Copyright © 2020 by Artur Laperla

Nunca te enfades con un gigante (Félix y Calcita 2) © 2020 by Penguin Random House Grupo Editorial Travessera de Gràcia, 47-49, Barcelona 08021, Spain

Graphic Universe™ is a trademark of Lerner Publishing Group, Inc.

All US rights reserved. No part of this book may be reproduced, stored in a retrieval system, or transmitted in any form or by any means—electronic, mechanical, photocopying, recording, or otherwise—without the prior written permission of Lerner Publishing Group, Inc., except for the inclusion of brief quotations in an acknowledged review.

Graphic Universe™
An imprint of Lerner Publishing Group, Inc.
241 First Avenue North
Minneapolis, MN 55401 USA

For reading levels and more information, look up this title at www.lernerbooks.com.

Main body text set in CCWildWords. Typeface provided by Comicraft.

Library of Congress Cataloging-in-Publication Data

Names: Laperla (Artist), author, illustrator. | MacTire, Norwyn, translator.
Title: Never make a giant mad / story and illustrations by Artur Laperla ; translation by Norwyn MacTire
Other titles: Nunca enfades a un gigante. English
Description: First American edition. | Minneapolis : Graphic Universe, 2022. | Series: Felix and Calcite ; book 2 | Audience: Ages 5-9 | Audience: Grades 2-3 | Summary: When Felix's favorite toy is lost in the land of trolls they must deal with Garganto, a giant who guards the path ahead.
Identifiers: LCCN 2021050333 (print) | LCCN 2021050334 (ebook) | ISBN 9781728416335 (library binding) | ISBN 9781728462912 (paperback) | ISBN 9781728460963 (ebook)
Subjects: CYAC: Graphic novels. | Trolls—Fiction. | Giants—Fiction. | Humorous stories. | LCGFT: Humorous comics. | Graphic novels.
Classification: LCC PZ7.7.L367 Ne 2022 (print) | LCC PZ7.7.L367 (ebook) | DDC 741.5/973—dc23/eng/20211110

LC record available at https://lccn.loc.gov/2021050333
LC ebook record available at https://lccn.loc.gov/2021050334

Manufactured in the United States of America
1-48883-49200-1/6/2022

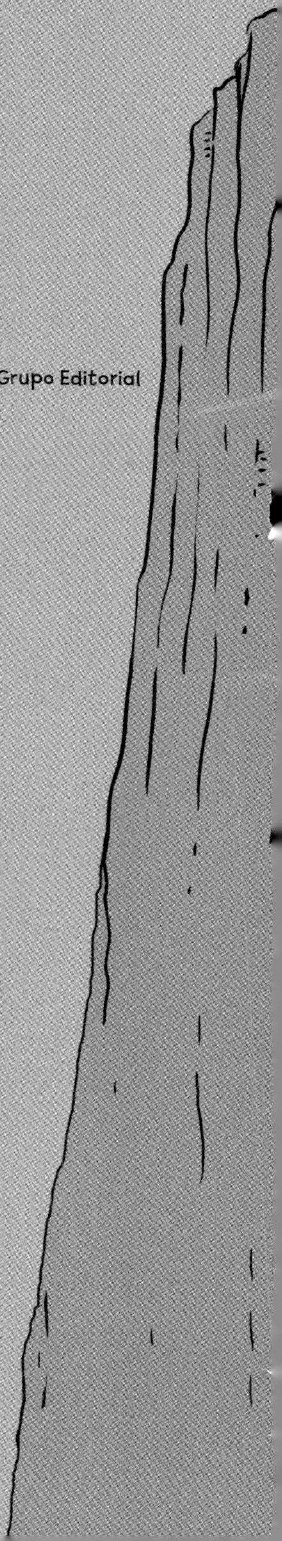

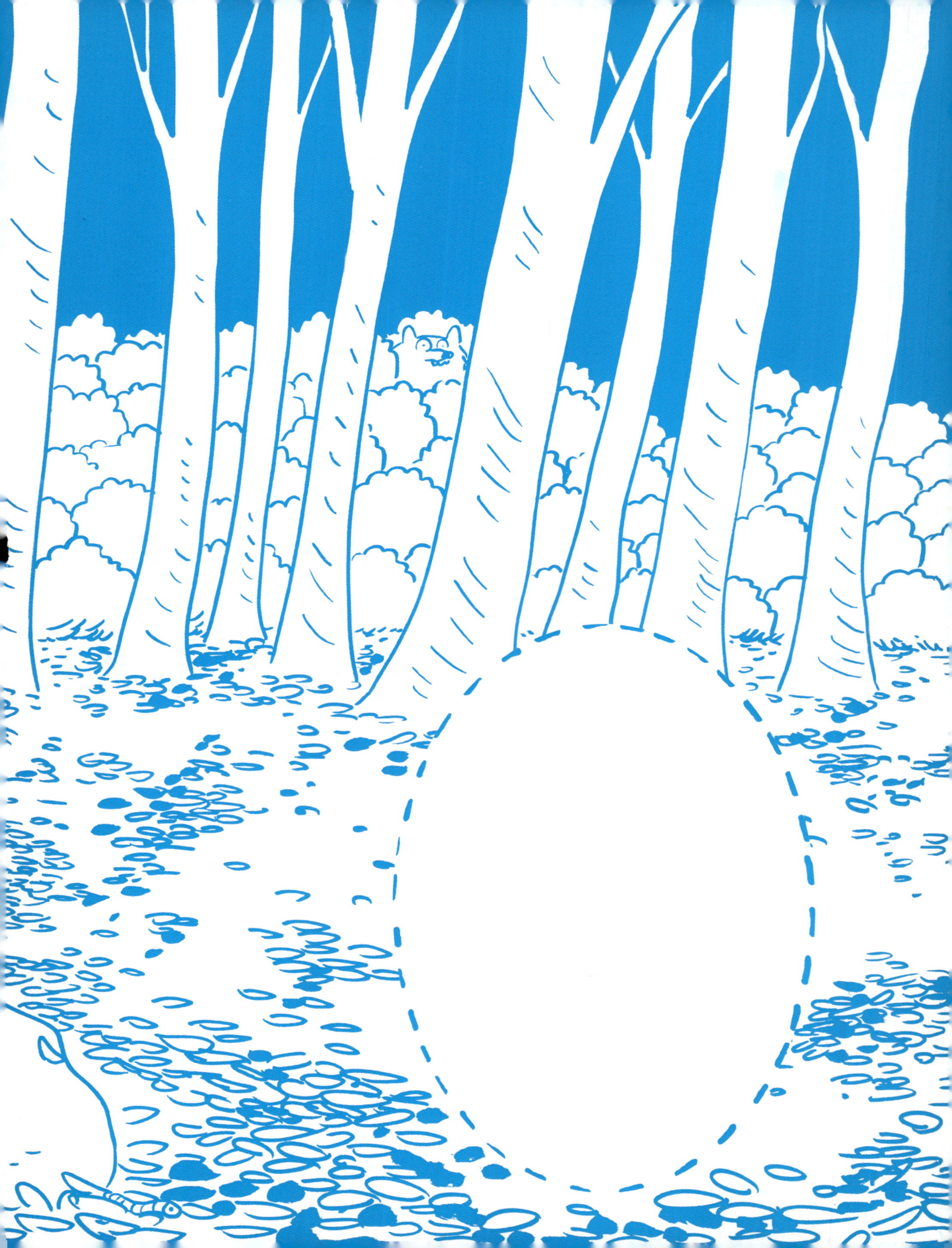